'I don't know why I told this story. I could just as well have told another. Perhaps some other time I'll be able to tell another. Living souls, you will see how alike they are'

SAMUEL BECKETT
Born 13 April 1906, Dublin
Died 22 December 1989, Paris

'The Expelled' [French, 1946] and 'First Love' [French, 1945]
first published in English in book form in *Four Novellas*,
John Calder, 1977.

SAMUEL BECKETT

The Expelled

TRANSLATED BY THE AUTHOR AND
RICHARD SEAVER

PENGUIN BOOKS

PENGUIN CLASSICS

Published by the Penguin Group
Penguin Books Ltd, 80 Strand, London WC2R ORL, England
Penguin Group (USA), Inc., 375 Hudson Street, New York, New York 10014, USA
Penguin Group (Canada), 90 Eglinton Avenue East, Suite 700, Toronto, Ontario,
Canada M4P 2Y3 (a division of Pearson Penguin Canada Inc.)
Penguin Ireland, 25 St Stephen's Green, Dublin 2, Ireland (a division of Penguin Books Ltd)
Penguin Group (Australia), 250 Camberwell Road, Camberwell, Victoria 3124, Australia
(a division of Pearson Australia Group Pty Ltd)
Penguin Books India Pvt Ltd, 11 Community Centre, Panchsheel Park,
New Delhi – 110 017, India
Penguin Group (NZ), 67 Apollo Drive, Rosedale, North Shore 0632, New Zealand
(a division of Pearson New Zealand Ltd)
Penguin Books (South Africa) (Pty) Ltd, 24 Sturdee Avenue, Rosebank, Johannesburg 2196,
South Africa

Penguin Books Ltd, Registered Offices: 80 Strand, London WC2R ORL, England

www.penguin.com

Selected from *First Love and Other Novellas*, published in Penguin Classics 2000
This edition published in Penguin Classics 2011

3

The Expelled copyright © Samuel Beckett, 1954
This translation copyright © Richard Seaver in collaboration with Samuel Beckett, 1967
First Love copyright © Les Éditions de Minuit, 1970
This translation copyright © Samuel Beckett, 1967

All rights reserved

Typeset by Jouve (UK), Milton Keynes
Printed in England by Clays Ltd, St Ives plc

ISBN: 978-0-141-19579-7

www.greenpenguin.co.uk

Penguin Books is committed to a sustainable future
for our business, our readers and our planet.
The book in your hands is made from paper
certified by the Forest Stewardship Council.

Contents

The Expelled

There were not many steps. I had counted them a thousand times, both going up and coming down, but the figure has gone from my mind. I have never known whether you should say one with your foot on the sidewalk, two with the following foot on the first step, and so on, or whether the sidewalk shouldn't count. At the top of the steps I fell foul of the same dilemma. In the other direction, I mean from top to bottom, it was the same, the word is not too strong. I did not know where to begin nor where to end, that's the truth of the matter. I arrived therefore at three totally different figures, without ever knowing which of them was right. And when I say that the figure has gone from my mind, I mean that none of the three figures is with me any more, in my mind. It is true that if I were to find, in my mind, where it is certainly to be found, one of these figures, I would find it and it alone, without being able to deduce from it the other two. And even were I to recover two,

I would not know the third. No, I would have to find all three, in my mind, in order to know all three. Memories are killing. So you must not think of certain things, of those that are dear to you, or rather you must think of them, for if you don't there is the danger of finding them, in your mind, little by little. That is to say, you must think of them for a while, a good while, every day several times a day, until they sink forever in the mud. That's an order.

After all it is not the number of steps that matters. The important thing to remember is that there were not many, and that I have remembered. Even for the child there were not many, compared to other steps he knew, from seeing them every day, from going up them and coming down, and from playing on them at knuckle-bones and other games the very names of which he has forgotten. What must it have been like then for the man I had overgrown into?

The fall was therefore not serious. Even as I fell I heard the door slam, which brought me a little comfort, in the midst of my fall. For that meant they were not pursuing me down into the street, with a stick, to beat me in full view of the passers-by. For if that had been their intention they would not have shut the door, but left it open, so that the persons assembled in the vestibule might enjoy my chastisement and be edified. So, for once, they had confined themselves to throwing me out and no more about it. I had time, before coming to rest in the gutter, to conclude this piece of reasoning.

Under these circumstances nothing compelled me to get up immediately. I rested my elbow on the sidewalk, funny the things you remember, settled my ear in the cup of my hand and began to reflect on my situation, notwithstanding its familiarity. But the sound, fainter but unmistakable, of the door slammed again, roused me from my reverie, in which already a whole landscape was taking form, charming with hawthorn and wild roses, most dreamlike, and made me look up in alarm, my hands flat on the sidewalk and my legs braced for flight. But it was merely my hat sailing towards me through the air, rotating as it came. I caught it and put it on. They were most correct, according to their god. They could have kept this hat, but it was not theirs, it was mine, so they gave it back to me. But the spell was broken.

How describe this hat? And why? When my head had attained I shall not say its definitive but its maximum dimensions, my father said to me, Come, son, we are going to buy your hat, as though it had pre-existed from time immemorial in a pre-established place. He went straight to the hat. I personally had no say in the matter, nor had the hatter. I have often wondered if my father's purpose was not to humiliate me, if he was

3

not jealous of me who was young and handsome, fresh at least, while he was already old and all bloated and purple. It was forbidden me, from that day forth, to go out bareheaded, my pretty brown hair blowing in the wind. Sometimes, in a secluded street, I took it off and held it in my hand, but trembling. I was required to brush it morning and evening. Boys my age with whom, in spite of everything, I was obliged to mix occasionally, mocked me. But I said to myself, It is not really the hat, they simply make merry at the hat because it is a little more glaring than the rest, for they have no finesse. I have always been amazed at my contemporaries' lack of finesse, I whose soul writhed from morning to night, in the mere quest of itself. But perhaps they were simply being kind, like those who make game of the hunchback's big nose. When my father died I could have got rid of this hat, there was nothing more to prevent me, but not I. But how describe it? Some other time, some other time.

I got up and set off. I forget how old I can have been. In what had just happened to me there was nothing in the least memorable. It was neither the cradle nor the grave of anything whatever. Or rather it resembled so many other cradles, so many other graves, that I'm lost. But I don't believe I exaggerate when I say that I was in the prime of life, what I believe is called the full

possession of one's faculties. Ah yes, them I possessed
all right. I crossed the street and turned back towards
the house that had just ejected me, I who never turned
back when leaving. How beautiful it was! There were
geraniums in the windows. I have brooded over geraniums for years. Geraniums are artful customers, but in
the end I was able to do what I liked with them. I have
always greatly admired the door of this house, up on
top of its little flight of steps. How describe it? It was a
massive green door, encased in summer in a kind of
green and white striped housing, with a hole for the
thunderous wrought-iron knocker and a slit for letters,
this latter closed to dust, flies and tits by a brass flap fit-
ted with springs. So much for that description. The
door was set between two pillars of the same colour,
the bell being on that to the right. The curtains were in
unexceptionable taste. Even the smoke rising from one
of the chimney-pots seemed to spread and vanish in the
air more sorrowful than the neighbours', and bluer. I
looked up at the third and last floor and saw my window outrageously open. A thorough cleansing was in
full swing. In a few hours they would close the window,
draw the curtains and spray the whole place with disin-
fectant. I knew them. I would have gladly died in that
house. In a sort of vision I saw the door open and my
feet come out.

I wasn't afraid to look, for I knew they were not spying on me from behind the curtains, as they could have done if they had wished. But I knew them. They had all gone back into their dens and resumed their occupations.

And yet I had done them no harm.

I did not know the town very well, scene of my birth and of my first steps in this world, and then of all the others, so many that I thought all trace of me was lost, but I was wrong. I went out so little! Now and then I would go to the window, part the curtains and look out. But then I hastened back to the depths of the room, where the bed was. I felt ill at ease with all this air about me, lost before the confusion of innumerable prospects. But I still knew how to act at this period, when it was absolutely necessary. But first I raised my eyes to the sky, whence cometh our help, where there are no roads, where you wander freely, as in a desert, and where nothing obstructs your vision, wherever you turn your eyes, but the limits of vision itself. When I was younger I thought life would be good in the middle of a plain and went to the Lüneburg heath. With the plain in my head I went to the heath. There were other heaths far less remote, but a voice kept saying to me, It's the Lüneburg heath you need. The element lüne must have had something to do with it. As it turned out the Lüneburg heath was most unsatisfactory, most unsatisfactory. I came home disappointed, and at the same time relieved. Yes, I don't know why, but I have never been disappointed, and I often was in the early days, without feeling at the same time, or a moment later, an undeniable relief.

I set off. What a gait. Stiffness of the lower limbs, as if nature had denied me knees, extraordinary splaying of the feet to right and left of the line of march. The trunk, on the contrary, as if by the effect of a compensatory mechanism, was as flabby as an old ragbag, tossing wildly to the unpredictable jolts of the pelvis. I have often tried to correct these defects, to stiffen my bust, flex my knees and walk with my feet in front of one another, for I had at least five or six, but it always ended in the same way, I mean with a loss of equilibrium, followed by a fall. A man must walk without paying attention to what he's doing, as he sighs, and when I walked without paying attention to what I was doing I walked in the way I have just described, and when I began to pay attention I managed a few steps of creditable execution and then fell. I decided therefore to be myself. This carriage is due, in my opinion, in part at least, to a certain leaning from which I have never been able to free myself completely and which left its stamp, as was only to be expected, on my impressionable years, those which govern the fabrication of character, I refer to the period which extends, as far as the eye can see, from the first totterings, behind a chair, to the third form, in which I concluded my studies. I had then the deplorable habit, having pissed in my trousers, or shat there, which I did fairly regularly early in the morning, about ten or half past ten, of persisting in going on and finishing my day as if nothing had happened. The very idea of changing my trousers, or of confiding in mother, who goodness knows asked nothing better than to help me, was unbearable, I don't know why, and till bedtime I dragged on with burning and stinking between my little thighs, or sticking to my bottom, the result of my incontinence. Whence this wary way of walking, with the legs stiff and wide apart, and this desperate rolling of the bust, no doubt intended to put people off the scent, to make them think I was full of gaiety and high spirits, without a care in the world, and to lend plausibility to my explanations concerning my nether rigidity, which I ascribed to hereditary rheumatism. My youthful ardour, in so far as I had any, spent itself in this effort, I became sour and mistrustful, a little before my time, in love with hiding and the prone position. Poor juvenile solutions, explaining nothing. No need then for caution, we may reason on to our heart's content, the fog won't lift.

The weather was fine. I advanced down the street, keeping as close as I could to the sidewalk. The widest sidewalk is never wide enough for me, once I set myself in motion, and I hate to inconvenience strangers. A policeman stopped me and said, The street for vehicles, the sidewalk for pedestrians. Like a bit of Old Testament. So I got back on the sidewalk, almost apologetically, and persevered there, in spite of an indescribable jostle, for a good twenty steps, till I had to fling myself to the ground to avoid crushing a child. He was wearing a little harness, I remember, with little bells, he must have taken himself for a pony, or a Clydesdale, why not. I would have crushed him gladly, I loathe children, and it would have been doing him a service, but I was afraid of reprisals. Everyone is a parent, that is what keeps you from hoping. One should reserve, on busy streets, special tracks for these nasty little creatures, their prams, hoops, sweets, scooters, skates, grandpas, grandmas, nannies, balloons and balls, all their foul little happiness in a word. I fell then, and brought down with me an old lady covered with spangles and lace, who must have weighed about sixteen stone. Her screams soon drew a crowd. I had high hopes she had broken her femur, old ladies break their femur easily, but not enough, not enough. I took advantage of the confusion to make off, muttering unintelligible oaths, as if I were the victim, and I was, but I couldn't have proved it. They never lynch children, babies, no matter what they do they are whitewashed in advance. I personally would lynch them with the utmost pleasure, I don't say I'd lend a hand, no, I am not a violent man, but I'd encourage the others and stand them drinks when it was done. But no sooner had I begun to reel on than I was stopped by a second policeman, similar in all respects to the first, so much so that I wondered whether it was not the same one. He pointed out to me that the sidewalk was for everyone, as if it was quite obvious that I could not be assimilated to that category. Would you like me, I said, without thinking for a single moment of Heraclitus, to get down in the gutter? Get down wherever you want, he said, but leave some room for others. If you can't bloody well get about like everyone else, he said, you'd do better to stay at home. It was exactly my feeling. And that he should attribute to me a home was no small satisfaction. At that moment a funeral passed, as sometimes happens. There was a great flurry of hats and at the same time a flutter of countless fingers. Personally if I were reduced to making the sign of the cross I would set my heart on doing it right, nose, navel, left nipple, right nipple. But the way they did it, slovenly and wild, he seemed crucified all of a heap, no dignity, his knees under his chin and his hands anyhow. The more fervent stopped dead and muttered. As for the policeman he stiffened to attention, closed his eyes and saluted.

Through the windows of the cabs I caught a glimpse of the mourners conversing with animation, no doubt scenes from the life of their late dear brother in Christ, or sister. I seem to have heard that the hearse trappings are not the same in both cases, but I never could find out what the difference consists in. The horses were farting and shitting as if they were going to the fair. I saw no one kneeling.

But with us the last journey is soon done, it is in vain you quicken your pace, the last cab containing the domestics soon leaves you behind, the respite is over, the bystanders go their ways, you may look to yourself again. So I stopped a third time, of my own free will, and entered a cab. Those I had just seen pass, crammed with people hotly arguing, must have made a strong impression on me. It's a big black box, rocking and swaying on its springs, the windows are small, you curl up in a corner, it smells musty. I felt my hat grazing the roof. A little later I leant forward and closed the windows. Then I sat down again with my back to the horse. I was dozing off when a voice made me start, the cabman's. He had opened the door, no doubt despairing of making himself heard through the window. All I saw was his moustache. Where to? he said. He had climbed down from his seat on purpose to ask me that. And I who thought I was far away already. I reflected, searching in my memory for the name of a street, or a monument. Is your cab for sale? I said. I added, Without the horse. What would I do with a horse? But what would I do with a cab? Could I as much as stretch out in it? Who would bring me food? To the Zoo, I said. It is rare for a capital to be without a Zoo. I added, Don't go too fast. He laughed. The suggestion that he might go too fast to the Zoo must have amused him. Unless it was the prospect of being cabless. Unless it was simply myself, my own person, whose presence in the cab must have transformed it, so much so that the cabman, seeing me there with my head in the shadows of the roof and my knees against the window, had wondered perhaps if it was really his cab, really a cab. He hastens to look at his horse, and is reassured. But does one ever know oneself why one laughs? His laugh in any case was brief, which suggested I was not the joke. He closed the door and climbed back to his seat. It was not long then before the horse got under way.

Yes, surprising though it may seem, I still had a little money at this time. The small sum my father had left me as a gift, with no restrictions, at his death, I still wonder if it wasn't stolen from me. Then I had none. And yet my life went on, and even in the way I wanted, up to a point. The great disadvantage of this condition, which might be defined as the absolute impossibility of all purchase, is that it compels you to bestir yourself. It is rare, for example, when you are completely penniless, that you can have food brought to you from time to time in your retreat. You are therefore obliged to go out and bestir yourself, at least one day a week. You can hardly have a home address under these circumstances, it's inevitable. It was therefore with a certain delay that I learnt they were looking for me, for an affair concerning me. I forget through what channel. I did not read the newspapers, nor do I remember having spoken with anyone during these years, except perhaps three or four times, on the subject of food. At any rate, I must have had wind of the affair one way or another, otherwise I would never have gone to see the lawyer, Mr Nidder, strange how one fails to forget certain names, and he would never have received me. He verified my identity. That took some time. I showed him the metal initials in the lining of my hat, they proved nothing but they increased the probabilities. Sign, he said. He played with a cylindrical ruler, you could have felled an ox with it. Count, he said. A young woman, perhaps venal, was present at this interview, as a witness no doubt. I stuffed the wad in my pocket. You shouldn't do that, he said. It occurred to me that he should have asked me to count before I signed, it would have been more in order. Where can I reach you, he said, if necessary? At the foot of the stairs I thought of something. Soon after I went back to ask him where this money came from, adding that I had a right to know. He gave me a woman's name that I've forgotten. Perhaps she had dandled me on her knees while I was still in swaddling clothes and there had been some lovey-dovey. Sometimes that suffices. I repeat, in swaddling clothes, for any later it would have been too late, for lovey-dovey. It is thanks to this money then that I still had a little. Very little. Divided by my life to come it was negligible, unless my conjectures were unduly pessimistic. I knocked on the partition beside my hat, right in the cabman's back if my calculations were correct. A cloud of dust rose from the upholstery. I took a stone from my pocket and knocked with the stone, until the cab stopped. I noticed that, unlike most vehicles, which slow down before stopping, the cab stopped dead. I waited. The whole cab shook. The cab-man, on his high seat, must have been listening. I saw the horse as with my eyes of flesh. It had not lapsed into the drooping attitude of its briefest halts, it remained alert, its ears pricked up. I looked out of the window, we were again in motion. I banged again on the parti-tion, until the cab stopped again. The cabman got down cursing from his seat. I lowered the window to prevent his opening the door. Faster, faster. He was redder than ever, purple in other words. Anger, or the rushing wind.

I told him I was hiring him for the day. He replied that he had a funeral at three o'clock. Ah the dead. I told him I had changed my mind and no longer wished to go to the Zoo. Let us not go to the Zoo, I said. He replied that it made no difference to him where we went, provided it wasn't too far, because of his beast. And they talk to us about the specificity of primitive peoples' speech. I asked him if he knew of an eating-house. I added, You'll eat with me. I prefer being with a regular customer in such places. There was a long table with two benches of exactly the same length on either side. Across the table he spoke to me of his life, of his wife, of his beast, then again of his life, of the atrocious life that was his, chiefly because of his character. He asked me if I realized what it meant to be out of doors in all weathers. I learnt there were still some cabmen who spent their day snug and warm inside their cabs on the rank, waiting for a customer to come and rouse them. Such a thing was possible in the past, but nowadays other methods were necessary, if a man was to have a little laid up at the end of his days. I described my situation to him, what I had lost and what I was looking for. We did our best, both of us, to understand, to explain. He understood that I had lost my room and needed another, but all the rest escaped him. He had taken it into his head, whence nothing could ever dislodge it, that I was looking for a furnished room. He took from his pocket an evening paper of the day before, or perhaps the day before that again, and proceeded to run through the advertisements, five or six of which he underlined with a tiny pencil, the same that hovered over the likely outsiders. He underlined no doubt those he would have underlined if he had been in my shoes, or perhaps those concentrated in the same area, because of his beast. I would only have confused him by saying that I could tolerate no furniture in my room except the bed, and that all the other pieces, and even the very night-table, had to be removed before I would consent to set foot in it. About three o'clock we roused the horse and set off again. The cabman suggested I climb up beside him on the seat, but for some time already I had been dreaming of the inside of the cab and I got back inside. We visited, methodically I hope, one after another, the addresses he had underlined. The short winter's day was drawing to a close. It seems to me sometimes that these are the only days I have ever known, and especially that most charming moment of all, just before night wipes them out. The addresses he had underlined, or rather marked with a cross, as common people do, proved fruitless one by one, and one by one he crossed them out with a diagonal stroke. Later he showed me the paper, advising me to keep it safe so as to be sure not to look again where I had already looked in vain. In spite of the closed windows, the creaking of the cab and the traffic noises, I heard him singing, all alone aloft on his seat. He had preferred me to a funeral, this was a fact which would endure forever. He sang, *She is far from the land where her young hero*, those are the only words I remember. At each stop he got down from his seat and helped me down from mine. I rang at the door he directed me to and sometimes I disappeared inside the house. It was a strange feeling, I remember, a house all about me again, after so long. He waited for me on the sidewalk and helped me climb back into the cab. I was sick and tired of this cabman. He clambered back to his seat and we set off again. At a certain moment there occurred this. He stopped. I shook off my torpor and made ready to get down. But he did not come to open the door and offer me his arm, so that I was obliged to get down by myself. He was lighting the lamps. I love oil lamps, in spite of their having been, with candles, and if I except the stars, the first lights I ever knew. I asked him if I might light the second lamp, since he had already lit the first himself. He gave me his box of matches, I swung open on its hinges the little convex glass, lit and closed at once, so that the wick might burn steady and bright, snug in its little house, sheltered from the wind. I had this joy. We saw nothing, by the light of these lamps, save the vague out-lines of the horse, but the others saw them from afar, two yellow glows sailing slowly through the air. When the equipage turned an eye could be seen, red or green as the case might be, a bossy rhomb as clear and keen as stained glass.

After we had verified the last address the cabman suggested bringing me to a hotel he knew where I would be comfortable. That makes sense, cabman, hotel, it's plausible. With his recommendation I would want for nothing. Every convenience, he said, with a wink. I place this conversation on the sidewalk, in front of the house from which I had just emerged. I remem-ber, beneath the lamp, the flank of the horse, hollow and damp, and on the handle of the door the cabman's hand in its woollen glove. The roof of the cab was on a level with my neck. I suggested we have a drink. The horse had neither eaten nor drunk all day. I mentioned this to the cabman, who replied that his beast would take no food till it was back in the stable. If it ate any-thing whatever, during work, were it but an apple or a lump of sugar, it would have stomach pains and colics that would root it to the spot and might even kill it. That was why he was compelled to tie its jaws together with a strap whenever for one reason or another he had to let it out of his sight, so that it would not have to

suffer from the kind hearts of the passers-by. After a few
drinks the cabman invited me to do his wife and him
the honour of spending the night in their home. It was
not far. Recollecting these emotions, with the cele-
brated advantage of tranquillity, it seems to me he did
nothing else, all that day, but turn about his lodging.
They lived above a stable, at the back of a yard. Ideal
location, I could have done with it. Having presented
me to his wife, extraordinarily full-bottomed, he left us.
She was manifestly ill at ease, alone with me. I could
understand her, I don't stand on ceremony on these
occasions. No reason for this to end or go on. Then let
it end. I said I would go down to the stable and sleep
there. The cabman protested. I insisted. He drew his
wife's attention to the pustule on top of my skull, for I
had removed my hat out of civility. He should have that
removed, she said. The cabman named a doctor he held
in high esteem who had rid him of an induration of the
seat. If he wants to sleep in the stable, said his wife, let
him sleep in the stable. The cabman took the lamp from
the table and preceded me down the stairs, or rather
ladder, which descended to the stable, leaving his wife
in the dark. He spread a horse blanket on the ground in
a corner on the straw and left me a box of matches in
case I needed to see clearly in the night. I don't remember what the horse was doing all this time. Stretched

out in the dark I heard the noise it made as it drank, a noise like no other, the sudden gallop of the rats and above me the muffled voices of the cabman and his wife as they criticized me. I held the box of matches in my hand, a big box of safety matches. I got up during the night and struck one. Its brief flame enabled me to locate the cab. I was seized, then abandoned, by the desire to set fire to the stable. I found the cab in the dark, opened the door, the rats poured out, I climbed in. As I settled down I noticed that the cab was no longer level, it was inevitable, with the shafts resting on the ground. It was better so, that allowed me to lie well back, with my feet higher than my head on the other seat. Several times during the night I felt the horse looking at me through the window and the breath of its nostrils. Now that it was unharnessed it must have been puzzled by my presence in the cab. I was cold, having forgotten to take the blanket, but not quite enough to go and get it. Through the window of the cab I saw the window of the stable, more and more clearly. I got out of the cab. It was not so dark now in the stable, I could make out the manger, the rack, the harness hanging, what else, buckets and brushes. I went to the door but couldn't open it. The horse didn't take its eyes off me. Don't horses ever sleep? It seemed to me the cabman should have tied it, to the manger for example. So I was obliged to leave by the window. It wasn't easy. But what is easy? I went out head first, my hands were flat on the ground of the yard while my legs were still thrashing to get clear of the frame. I remember the tufts of grass on which I pulled with both hands, in my effort to extricate myself. I should have taken off my greatcoat and thrown it through the window, but that would have meant thinking of it. No sooner had I left the yard than I thought of something. Weakness. I slipped a banknote in the matchbox, went back to the yard and placed the box on the sill of the window through which I had just come. The horse was at the window. But after I had taken a few steps in the street I returned to the yard and took back my banknote. I left the matches, they were not mine. The horse was still at the window. I was sick and tired of this cabhorse. Dawn was just breaking. I did not know where I was. I made towards the rising sun, towards where I thought it should rise, the quicker to come into the light. I would have liked a sea horizon, or a desert one. When I am abroad in the morning I go to meet the sun, and in the evening, when I am abroad, I follow it, till I am down among the dead. I don't know why I told this story. I could just as well have told another. Perhaps some other time I'll be able to tell another. Living souls, you will see how alike they are.

First Love

I associate, rightly or wrongly, my marriage with the death of my father, in time. That other links exist, on other levels, between these two affairs, is not impossible. I have enough trouble as it is in trying to say what I think I know.

I visited, not so long ago, my father's grave, that I do know, and noted the date of his death, of his death alone, for that of his birth had no interest for me, on that particular day. I set out in the morning and was back by night, having lunched lightly in the graveyard. But some days later, wishing to know his age at death, I had to return to the grave, to note the date of his birth. These two limiting dates I then jotted down on a piece of paper, which I now carry about with me. I am thus in a position to affirm that I must have been about twenty-five at the time of my marriage. For the date of my own birth, I repeat, my own birth, I have never forgotten, I never had to note it down, it remains graven in my memory, the year at least, in figures that life will not easily erase. The day itself comes back to me, when I put my mind to it, and I often celebrate it, after my fashion, I don't say each time it comes back, for it comes back too often, but often.

Personally I have no bone to pick with graveyards, I take the air there willingly, perhaps more willingly than elsewhere, when take the air I must. The smell of corpses, distinctly perceptible under those of grass and humus mingled, I do not find unpleasant, a trifle on the sweet side perhaps, a trifle heady, but how infinitely preferable to what the living emit, their feet, teeth, armpits, arses, sticky foreskins and frustrated ovules. And when my father's remains join in, however modestly, I can almost shed a tear. The living wash in vain, in vain perfume themselves, they stink. Yes, as a place for an outing, when out I must, leave me my graveyards and keep – you – to your public parks and beauty-spots. My sandwich, my banana, taste sweeter when I'm sitting on a tomb, and when the time comes to piss again, as it so often does, I have my pick. Or I wander, hands clasped behind my back, among the slabs, the flat, the leaning and the upright, culling the inscriptions. Of these I never weary, there are always three or four of such drollery that I have to hold on to the cross, or the stele, or the angel, so as not to fall. Mine I composed long since and am still pleased with it, tolerably pleased. My other writings are no sooner dry than they revolt me, but my epitaph still meets with my approval. There is little chance unfortunately of its ever being reared above the skull that conceived it, unless the State takes up the matter. But to be unearthed I must first be found, and I greatly fear those gentlemen will have as much trouble finding me dead as alive. So I hasten to record it here and now, while there is yet time:

> Hereunder lies the above who up below
> So hourly died that he lived on till now.

The second and last or rather latter line limps a little perhaps, but that is no great matter, I'll be forgiven more than that when I'm forgotten. Then with a little luck you hit on a genuine interment, with real live mourners and the odd relict trying to throw herself into the pit. And nearly always that charming business with the dust, though in my experience there is nothing less dusty than holes of this type, verging on muck for the most part, nor anything particularly powdery about the deceased, unless he happened to have died, or she, by fire. No matter, their little gimmick with the dust is charming. But my father's yard was not amongst my favourites. To begin with it was too remote, way out in the wilds of the country on the side of a hill, and too small, far too small, to go on with. Indeed it was almost full, a few more widows and they'd be turning them away. I infinitely preferred Ohlsdorf, particularly the Linne section, on Prussian soil, with its nine hundred acres of corpses packed tight, though I knew no one there, except by reputation the wild animal collector Hagenbeck. A lion, if I remember right, is carved on his monument, death must have had for Hagenbeck the countenance of a lion. Coaches ply to and fro, crammed with widows, widowers, orphans and the like. Groves, grottoes, artificial lakes with swans, offer consolation to the inconsolable. It was December, I had never felt so cold, the eel soup lay heavy on my stomach, I was afraid I'd die, I turned aside to vomit, I envied them.

But to pass on to less melancholy matters, on my father's death I had to leave the house. It was he who wanted me in the house. He was a strange man. One day he said, Leave him alone, he's not disturbing anyone. He didn't know I was listening. This was a view he must have often voiced, but the other times I wasn't by. They would never let me see his will, they simply said he had left me such a sum. I believed then and still believe he had stipulated in his will that I be left the room I had occupied in his lifetime and for food to be brought me there, as hitherto. He may even have given this the force of condition precedent. Presumably he liked to feel me under his roof, otherwise he would not have opposed my eviction. Perhaps he merely pitied me. But somehow I think not. He should have left me the entire house, then I'd have been all right, the others too for that matter, I'd have summoned them and said, Stay, stay by all means, your home is here. Yes, he was properly had, my poor father, if his purpose was really to go on protecting me from beyond the tomb. With regard to the money it is only fair to say they gave it to me without delay, on the very day following the inhumation. Perhaps they were legally bound to. I said to them, Keep this money and let me live on here, in my room, as in Papa's lifetime. I added, God rest his soul, in the hope of melting them. But they refused. I offered to place myself at their disposal, a few hours every day, for the little odd maintenance jobs every dwelling requires, if it is not to crumble away. Pottering is still just possible, I don't know why. I proposed in particular to look after the hothouse. There I would have gladly whiled away the hours, in the heat, tending the tomatoes, hyacinths, pinks and seedlings. My father and I alone, in that household, understood tomatoes. But they refused. One day, on my return from stool, I found my room locked and my belongings in a heap before the door. This will give you some idea how constipated I was, at this juncture. It was, I am now convinced, anxiety constipation. But was I genuinely constipated? Somehow I think not. Softly, softly. And yet I must have been, for how otherwise account for those long, those cruel sessions in the necessary house? At such times I never read, any more than at other times, never gave way to revery or meditation, just gazed dully at the almanac hanging from a nail before my eyes, with its chromo of a bearded stripling in the midst of sheep, Jesus no doubt, parted the cheeks with both hands and strained, heave! ho! heave! ho!, with the motions of one tugging at the oar, and only one thought in my mind, to be back in my room and flat on my back again. What can that have been but constipation? Or am I confusing it with diarrhoea? It's all a muddle in my head, graves and nuptials and the different varieties of motion. Of my scanty belongings they had made a little heap, on the floor, against the door. I can still see that little heap, in the kind of recess full of shadow between the landing and my room. It was in this narrow space, guarded on three sides only, that I had to change, I mean exchange my dressing-gown and nightgown for my travelling costume, I mean shoes, socks, trousers, shirt, coat, greatcoat and hat, I can think of nothing else. I tried other doors, turning the knobs and pushing, or pulling, before I left the house, but none yielded. I think if I'd found one open I'd have barricaded myself in the room, nothing less than gas would have dislodged me. I felt the house crammed as usual, the usual pack, but saw no one. I imagined them in their various rooms, all bolts drawn, every sense on the alert. Then the rush to the window, each holding back a little, hidden by the curtain, at the sound of the street door closing behind me, I should have left it open. Then the doors fly open and out they pour, men, women and children, and the voices, the sighs, the smiles, the hands, the keys in the hands, the blessed relief, the precautions rehearsed, if this then that, but if that then this, all clear and joy in every heart, come let's eat, the fumigation can wait. All imagination to be sure, I was already on my way, things may have passed quite differently, but who cares how things pass, provided they pass. All those lips that had kissed me, those hearts that had loved me (it is with the heart one loves, is it not, or am I confusing it with something else?), those hands that had played with mine and those minds that had almost made their own of me! Humans are truly strange. Poor Papa, a nice mug he must have felt that day if he could see me, see us, a nice mug on my account I mean. Unless in his great disembodied wisdom he saw further than his son whose corpse was not yet quite up to scratch.

But to pass on to less melancholy matters, the name

of the woman with whom I was soon to be united was Lulu. So at least she assured me and I can't see what interest she could have had in lying to me, on this score. Of course one can never tell. She also disclosed her family name, but I've forgotten it. I should have made a note of it, on a piece of paper, I hate to forget a proper name. I met her on a bench, on the bank of the canal, one of the canals, for our town boasts two, though I never knew which was which. It was a well-situated bench, backed by a mound of solid earth and garbage, so that my rear was covered. My flanks too, partially, thanks to a pair of venerable trees, more than venerable, dead, at either end of the bench. It was no doubt these trees one fine day, aripple with all their foliage, that had sown the idea of a bench, in someone's fancy. To the fore, a few yards away, flowed the canal, if canals flow, don't ask me, so that from that quarter too the risk of surprise was small. And yet she surprised me. I lay stretched out, the night being warm, gazing up through the bare boughs interlocking high above me, where the trees clung together for support, and through the drifting cloud, at a patch of starry sky as it came and went. Shove up, she said. My first movement was to go, but my fatigue, and my having nowhere to go, dissuaded me from acting on it. So I drew back my feet a little way and she sat. Nothing more passed between us that evening and she soon took herself off, without another word. All she had done was sing, beneath her breath, as to herself, and without the words fortunately, some old folk songs, and so disjointedly, skipping from one to another and finishing none, that even I found it strange. The voice, though out of tune, was not unpleasant. It breathed of a soul too soon wearied ever to conclude, that perhaps least arse-aching soul of all. The bench itself was soon more than she could bear and as for me, one look had been enough for her. Whereas in reality she was a most tenacious woman. She came back next day and the day after and all went off more or less as before. Perhaps a few words were exchanged. The next day it was raining and I felt in security. Wrong again. I asked her if she was resolved to disturb me every evening. I disturb you? she said. I felt her eyes on me. They can't have seen much, two eyelids at the most, with a hint of nose and brow, darkly, because of the dark. I thought we were easy, she said. You disturb me, I said, I can't stretch out with you there. The collar of my greatcoat was over my mouth and yet she heard me. Must you stretch out? she said. The mistake one makes is to speak to people. You have only to put your feet on my knees, she said. I didn't wait to be asked twice, under my miserable calves I felt her fat thighs. She began stroking my ankles. I considered kicking her in the cunt. You speak to people about stretching out and they immediately see a body at full length. What mattered to me in my dispeopled kingdom, that in regard to which the disposition of my carcass was the merest and most futile of accidents, was supineness in the mind, the dulling of the self and of that residue of execrable frippery known as the non-self and even the world, for short. But man is still today, at the age of twenty-five, at the mercy of an erection, physically too, from time to time, it's the common lot, even I was not immune, if that may be called an erection. It did not escape her naturally, women smell a rigid phallus ten miles away and wonder, How on earth did he spot me from there? One is no longer oneself, on such occasions, and it is painful to be no longer oneself, even more painful if possible than when one is. For when one is one knows what to do to be less so, whereas when one is not one is any old one irredeemably. What goes by the name of love is banishment, with now and then a postcard from the homeland, such is my considered opinion, this evening. When she had finished and my self been resumed, mine own, the mitigable, with the help of a brief torpor, it was alone. I sometimes wonder if that is not all invention, if in reality things did not take quite a different course, one I had no choice but to forget. And yet her image remains bound, for me, to that of the bench, not the bench by day, nor yet the bench by night, but the bench at evening, in such sort that to speak of the bench, as it appeared to me at evening, is to speak of her, for me. That proves nothing, but there is nothing I wish to prove. On the subject of the bench by day no words need be wasted, it never knew me, gone before morning and never back till dusk. Yes, in the daytime I foraged for food and marked down likely cover. Were you to inquire, as undoubtedly you itch, what I had done with the money my father had left me, the answer would be I had done nothing with it but leave it lie in my pocket. For I knew I would not be always young, and that summer does not last for ever either, nor even autumn, my mean soul told me so. In the end I told her I'd had enough. She disturbed me exceedingly, even absent. Indeed she still disturbs me, but no worse now than the rest. And it matters nothing to me now, to be disturbed, or so little, what does it mean, disturbed, and what would I do with myself if I wasn't? Yes, I've changed my system, it's the winning one at last, for the ninth or tenth time, not to mention not long now, not long till curtain down, on disturbers and disturbed, no more tattle about that, all that, her and the others, the shitball and heaven's high halls. So you don't want me to come any more, she said. It's incredible the way they repeat what you've just said to them, as if they risked faggot and fire in believing their ears. I told her to come just the odd time. I didn't understand women at that period. I still don't for that matter. Nor men either. Nor animals either. What I understand best, which is not saying much, are my pains. I think them through daily, it doesn't take long, thought moves so fast, but they are not only in my thought, not all. Yes, there are moments, particularly in the afternoon, when I go all syncretist, à la Reinhold. What equilibrium! But even them, my pains, I understand ill. That must come from my not being all pain and nothing else. There's the rub. Then they recede, or I, till they fill me with amaze and wonder, seen from a better planet. Not often, but I ask no more. Catch-cony life! To be nothing but pain, how that would simplify matters! Omnidolent! Impious dream. I'll tell them to you some day none the less, if I think of it, if I can, my strange pains, in detail, distinguishing between the different kinds, for the sake of clarity, those of the mind, those of the heart or emotional conative, those of the soul (none prettier than these) and finally those of the frame proper, first the inner or latent, then those affecting the surface, beginning with the hair and scalp and moving methodically down, without haste, all the way down to the feet beloved of the corn, the cramp, the kibe, the bunion, the hammer toe, the nail ingrown, the fallen arch, the common blain, the club foot, duck foot, goose foot, pigeon foot, flat foot, trench foot and other curiosities. And I'll tell by the same token, for those kind enough to listen, in accordance with a system whose inventor I forget, of those instants when, neither drugged, nor drunk, nor in ecstasy, one feels nothing. Next of course she desired to know what I meant by the odd time, that's what you get for opening your mouth. Once a week? Once in ten days? Once a fortnight? I replied less often, far less often, less often to the point of no more if she could, and if she could not the least often possible. And the next day (what is more) I abandoned the bench, less I must confess on her account than on its, for the site no longer answered my requirements, modest though they were, now that the air was beginning to strike chill, and for other reasons better not wasted on cunts like you, and took refuge in a deserted cowshed marked on one of my forays. It stood in the corner of a field richer on the surface in nettles than in grass and in mud than in nettles, but whose subsoil was perhaps possessed of exceptional qualities. It was in this byre, littered with dry and hollow cowclaps subsiding with a sigh at the poke of my finger, that for the first time in my life, and I would not hesitate to say the last if I had not to husband my cyanide, I had to contend with a feeling which gradually assumed, to my dismay, the dread name of love. What constitutes the charm of our country, apart of course from its scant population, and this without help of the meanest contraceptive, is that all is derelict, with the sole exception of history's ancient faeces. These are ardently sought after, stuffed and carried in procession. Wherever nauseated time has dropped a nice fat turd you will find our patriots, sniffing it up on all fours, their faces on fire. Elysium of the roofless. Hence my happiness at last. Lie down, all seems to say, lie down and stay down. I see no connexion between these remarks. But that one exists, and even more than one, I have little doubt, for my part. But what? Which? Yes, I loved her, it's the name I gave, still give alas, to what I was doing then. I had nothing to go by, having never loved before, but of course had heard of the thing, at home, in school, in brothel and at church, and read romances, in prose and verse, under the guidance of my tutor, in six or seven languages, both dead and living, in which it was handled at length. I was therefore in a position, in spite of all, to put a label on what I was about when I found myself inscribing the letters of Lulu in an old heifer pat or flat on my face in the mud under the moon trying to tear up the nettles by the roots. They were giant nettles some full three foot high, to tear them up assuaged my pain, and yet it's not like me to do that to weeds, on the contrary, I'd smother them in manure if I had any. Flowers are a different matter. Love brings out the worst in man and no error. But what kind of love was this, exactly? Love-passion? Somehow I think not. That's the priapic one, is it not? Or is this a different variety? There are so many, are there not? All equally if not more delicious, are they not? Platonic love, for example, there's another just occurs to me. It's disinterested. Perhaps I loved her with a platonic love? But somehow I think not. Would I have been tracing her name in old cowshit if my love had been pure and disinterested? And with my devil's finger into the bargain, which I then sucked. Come now! My thoughts were all of Lulu, if that doesn't give you some idea nothing will. Anyhow I'm sick and tired of this name Lulu, I'll give her another, more like her, Anna for example, it's not more like her but no matter. I thought of Anna then, I who had learnt to think of nothing, nothing except my pains, a quick think through, and of what steps to take not to perish off-hand of hunger, or cold, or shame, but never on any account of living beings as such (I wonder what that means) whatever I may have said, or may still say, to the contrary or otherwise, on this subject. But I have always spoken, no doubt always shall, of things that never existed, or that existed if you insist, no doubt always will, but not with the existence I ascribe to them. Kepis, for example, exist beyond a doubt, indeed there is little hope of their ever disappearing, but personally I never wore a kepi. I wrote somewhere, They gave me . . . a hat. Now the truth is they never gave me a hat, I have always had my own hat, the one my father gave me, and I have never had any other hat than that hat. I may add it has followed me to the grave. I thought of Anna then, long long sessions, twenty minutes, twenty-five minutes and even as long as half an hour daily. I obtain these figures by the addition of other, lesser figures. That must have been my way of loving. Are we to infer from this I loved her with that intellectual love which drew from me such drivel, in another place? Somehow I think not. For had my love been of this kind would I have stooped to inscribe the letters of Anna in time's forgotten cowpats? To divellicate urtica *plenis manibus*? And felt, under my tossing head, her thighs to bounce like so many demon bolsters? Come now! In order to put an end, to try and put an end, to this plight, I returned one evening to the bench, at the hour she had used to join me there. There was no sign of her and I waited in vain. It was December already, if not January, and the cold was seasonable, that is to say reasonable, like all that is seasonable. But one is the hour of the dial, and another that of changing air and sky, and another yet again the heart's. To this thought, once back in the straw, I owed an excellent night. The next day I was earlier to the bench, much

earlier, night having barely fallen, winter night, and yet
too late, for she was there already, on the bench, under
the boughs tinkling with rime, her back to the frosted
mound, facing the icy water. I told you she was a highly
tenacious woman. I felt nothing. What interest could
she have in pursuing me thus? I asked her, without sitting down, stumping to and fro. The cold had embossed
the path. She replied she didn't know. What could she
see in me, would she kindly tell me that at least, if she
could. She replied she couldn't. She seemed warmly
clad, her hands buried in a muff. As I looked at this
muff, I remember, tears came to my eyes. And yet I forget what colour it was. The state I was in then! I have
always wept freely, without the least benefit to myself,
till recently. If I had to weep this minute I could squeeze
till I was blue, I'm convinced not a drop would fall. The
state I am in now! It was things made me weep. And yet
I felt no sorrow. When I found myself in tears for no
apparent reason it meant I had caught sight of something unbeknownst. So I wonder if it was really the
muff that evening, if it was not rather the path, so iron
hard and bossy as perhaps to feel like cobbles to my
tread, or some other thing, some chance thing glimpsed
below the threshold, that so unmanned me. As for her,
I might as well never have laid eyes on her before. She
sat all huddled and muffled up, her head sunk, the muff

39

with her hands in her lap, her legs pressed tight together, her heels clear of the ground. Shapeless, ageless, almost lifeless, it might have been anything or anyone, an old woman or a little girl. And the way she kept on saying, I don't know, I can't. I alone did not know and could not. Is it on my account you came? I said. She managed yes to that. Well here I am, I said. And I? Had I not come on hers? Here we are, I said. I sat down beside her but sprang up again immediately as though scalded. I longed to be gone, to know if it was over. But before going, to be on the safe side, I asked her to sing me a song. I thought at first she was going to refuse, I mean simply not sing, but no, after a moment she began to sing and sang for some time, all the time the same song it seemed to me, without change of attitude. I did not know the song, I had never heard it before and shall never hear it again. It had something to do with lemon trees, or orange trees, I forget, that is all I remember, and for me that is no mean feat, to remember it had something to do with lemon trees, or orange trees, I forget, for of all the other songs I have ever heard in my life, and I have heard plenty, it being apparently impossible, physically impossible short of being deaf, to get through this world, even my way, without hearing singing, I have retained nothing, not a word, not a note, or so few words, so few notes, that, that what, that nothing, this sentence has gone on long enough. Then I started to go and as I went I heard her singing another song, or perhaps more verses of the same, fainter and fainter the further I went, then no more, either because she had come to an end or because I was gone too far to hear her. To have to harbour such a doubt was something I preferred to avoid, at that period. I lived of course in doubt, on doubt, but such trivial doubts as this, purely somatic as some say, were best cleared up without delay, they could nag at me like gnats for weeks on end. So I retraced my steps a little way and stopped. At first I heard nothing, then the voice again, but only just, so faintly did it carry. First I didn't hear it, then I did, I must therefore have begun hearing it, at a certain point, but no, there was no beginning, the sound emerged so softly from the silence and so resembled it. When the voice ceased at last I approached a little nearer, to make sure it had really ceased and not merely been lowered. Then in despair, saying, No knowing, no knowing, short of being beside her, bent over her, I turned on my heel and went, for good, full of doubt. But some weeks later, even more dead than alive than usual I returned to the bench, for the fourth or fifth time since I had abandoned it, at roughly the same hour, I mean roughly the same sky, no, I don't mean that either, for it's always the same sky and never the same sky, what words are there for that, none

I know, period. She wasn't there, then suddenly she was, I don't know how, I didn't see her come, nor hear her, all ears and eyes though I was. Let us say it was raining, nothing like a change, if only of weather. She had her umbrella up, naturally, what an outfit. I asked if she came every evening. No, she said, just the odd time. The bench was soaking wet, we paced up and down, not daring to sit. I took her arm, out of curiosity, to see if it would give me pleasure, it gave me none, I let it go. But why these particulars? To put off the evil hour. I saw her face a little clearer, it seemed normal to me, a face like millions of others. The eyes were crooked, but I didn't know that till later. It looked neither young nor old, the face, as though stranded between the vernal and the sere. Such ambiguity I found difficult to bear, at that period. As to whether it was beautiful, the face, or had once been beautiful, or could conceivably become beautiful, I confess I could form no opinion. I had seen faces in photographs I might have found beautiful had I known even vaguely in what beauty was supposed to consist. And my father's face, on his death-bolster, had seemed to hint at some form of aesthetics relevant to man. But the faces of the living, all grimace and flush, can they be described as objects? I admired in spite of the dark, in spite of my fluster, the way still or scarcely flowing water reaches up, as though athirst, to that falling from the sky. She asked if I would like her to sing something. I replied no, I would like her to say something. I thought she would say she had nothing to say, it would have been like her, and so was agreeably surprised when she said she had a room, most agreeably surprised, though I suspected as much. Who has not a room? Ah I hear the clamour. I have two rooms, she said. Just how many rooms do you have? I said. She said she had two rooms and a kitchen. The premises were expanding steadily, given time she would remember a bathroom. Is it two rooms I heard you say? I said. Yes, she said. Adjacent? I said. At last conversation worthy of the name. Separated by the kitchen, she said. I asked her why she had not told me before. I must have been beside myself, at this period. I did not feel easy when I was with her, but at least free to think of something else than her, of the old trusty things, and so little by little, as down steps towards a deep, of nothing. And I knew that away from her I would forfeit this freedom.

There were in fact two rooms, separated by a kitchen, she had not lied to me. She said I should have fetched my things. I explained I had no things. It was at the top of an old house, with a view of the mountains for those who cared. She lit an oil-lamp. You have no current? I said. No, she said, but I have running water and gas. Ha, I said, you have gas. She began to undress.

When at their wit's end they undress, no doubt the wisest course. She took off everything, with a slowness fit to enflame an elephant, except her stockings, calculated presumably to bring my concupiscence to the boil. It was then I noticed the squint. Fortunately she was not the first naked woman to have crossed my path, so I could stay, I knew she would not explode. I asked to see the other room which I had not yet seen. If I had seen it already I would have asked to see it again. Will you not undress? she said. Oh you know, I said, I seldom undress. It was the truth, I was never one to undress indiscriminately. I often took off my boots when I went to bed, I mean when I composed myself (composed!) to sleep, not to mention this or that outer garment according to the outer temperature. She was therefore obliged, out of common savoir faire, to throw on a wrap and light me the way. We went via the kitchen. We could just as well have gone via the corridor, as I realized later, but we went via the kitchen, I don't know why, perhaps it was the shorter way. I surveyed the room with horror. Such density of furniture defeats imagination. Not a doubt, I must have seen that room somewhere. What's this? I cried. The parlour, she said. The parlour! I began putting out the furniture through the door to the corridor. She watched, in sorrow I suppose, but not necessarily. She asked me what I was doing. She can't have expected an answer. I put it out piece by piece, and even two at a time, and stacked it all up in the corridor, against the outer wall. There were hundreds of pieces, large and small, in the end they blocked the door, making egress impossible, and *a fortiori* ingress, to and from the corridor. The door could be opened and closed, since it opened inwards, but had become impassable. To put it mildly. At least take off your hat, she said. I'll treat of my hat some other time perhaps. Finally the room was empty but for a sofa and some shelves fixed to the wall. The former I dragged to the back of the room, near the door, and next day took down the latter and put them out, in the corridor, with the rest. As I was taking them down, strange memory, I heard the word fibrome, or brone, I don't know which, never knew, never knew what it meant and never had the curiosity to find out. The things one recalls! And records! When all was in order at last I dropped on the sofa. She had not raised her little finger to help me. I'll get sheets and blankets, she said. But I wouldn't hear of sheets. You couldn't draw the curtain? I said. The window was frosted over. The effect was not white, because of the night, but faintly luminous none the less. This faint cold sheen, though I lay with my feet towards the door, was more than I could bear. I suddenly rose and changed the position of the sofa, that is to say turned it round so that the back, hitherto against the wall, was now on the out-side and consequently the front, or way in, on the inside. Then I climbed back, like a dog into its basket. I'll leave you the lamp, she said, but I begged her to take it with her. And suppose you need something in the night, she said. She was going to start quibbling again, I could feel it. Do you know where the convenience is? she said. She was right, I was forgetting. To relieve oneself in bed is enjoyable at the time, but soon a source of discomfort. Give me a chamber-pot, I said. But she did not possess one. I have a close-stool of sorts, she said. I saw the grandmother on it, sitting up very stiff and grand, hav-ing just purchased it, pardon, picked it up, at a charity sale, or perhaps won it in a raffle, a period piece, and now trying it out, doing her best rather, almost wishing someone could see her. That's the idea, procrastinate. Any old recipient, I said, I don't have the flux. She came back with a kind of saucepan, not a true saucepan for it had no handle, it was oval in shape with two lugs and a lid. My stewpan, she said. I don't need the lid, I said. You don't need the lid? she said. If I had needed the lid she would have said, You need the lid? I drew this utensil down under the blanket, I like something in my hand when sleeping, it reassures me, and my hat was still wringing. I turned to the wall. She caught up the lamp off the mantelpiece where she had set it down, that's the idea, every particular, it flung her waving shadow over me, I thought she was off, but no, she came stooping down towards me over the sofa back. All family possessions, she said. I in her shoes would have tiptoed away, but not she, not a stir. Already my love was waning, that was all that mattered. Yes, already I felt better, soon I'd be up to the slow descents again, the long submersions, so long denied me through her fault. And I had only just moved in! Try and put me out now, I said. I seemed not to grasp the meaning of these words, nor even hear the brief sound they made, till some seconds after having uttered them. I was so unused to speech that my mouth would sometimes open, of its own accord, and vent some phrase or phrases, grammatically unexceptionable but entirely devoid if not of meaning, for on close inspection they would reveal one, and even several, at least of foundation. But I heard each word no sooner spoken. Never had my voice taken so long to reach me as on this occasion. I turned over on my back to see what was going on. She was smiling. A little later she went away, taking the lamp with her. I heard her steps in the kitchen and then the door of her room close behind her. Why behind her? I was alone at last, in the dark at last. Enough about that. I thought I was all set for a good night, in spite of the strange surroundings, but no, my night was most agitated. I woke

47

next morning quite worn out, my clothes in disorder, the blanket likewise, and Anna beside me, naked naturally. One shudders to think of her exertions. I still had the stewpan in my grasp. It had not served. I looked at my member. If only it could have spoken! Enough about that. It was my night of love.

Gradually I settled down, in this house. She brought my meals at the appointed hours, looked in now and then to see if all was well and make sure I needed nothing, emptied the stewpan once a day and did out the room once a month. She could not always resist the temptation to speak to me, but on the whole gave me no cause to complain. Sometimes I heard her singing in her room, the song traversed her door, then the kitchen, then my door, and in this way won to me, faint but indisputable. Unless it travelled by the corridor. This did not greatly incommode me, this occasional sound of singing. One day I asked her to bring me a hyacinth, live, in a pot. She brought it and put it on the mantelpiece, now the only place in my room to put things, unless you put them on the floor. Not a day passed without my looking at it. At first all went well, it even put forth a bloom or two, then it gave up and was soon no more than a limp stem hung with limp leaves. The bulb, half clear of the clay as though in search of oxygen, smelt foul. She wanted to remove it, but I told

her to leave it. She wanted to get me another, but I
told her I didn't want another. I was more seriously disturbed by other sounds, stifled giggles and groans,
which filled the dwelling at certain hours of the night,
and even of the day. I had given up thinking of her,
quite given up, but still I needed silence, to live my life.
In vain I tried to listen to such reasonings as that air is
made to carry the clamours of the world, including
inevitably much groan and giggle, I obtained no relief.
I couldn't make out if it was always the same gent or
more than one. Lovers' groans are so alike, and lovers'
giggles. I had such horror then of these paltry perplexi-
ties that I always fell into the same error, that of seeking
to clear them up. It took me a long time, my lifetime so
to speak, to realize that the colour of an eye half seen, or
the source of some distant sound, are closer to Giudecca
in the hell of unknowing than the existence of God, or
the origins of protoplasm, or the existence of self, and
even less worthy than these to occupy the wise. It's a bit
much, a lifetime, to achieve this consoling conclusion, it
doesn't leave you much time to profit by it. So a fat lot
of help it was when, having put the question to her,
I was told they were clients she received in rotation. I
could obviously have got up and gone to look through
the keyhole. But what can you see, I ask you, through
holes the likes of those? So you live by prostitution,

I said. We live by prostitution, she said. You couldn't ask them to make less noise? I said, as if I believed her. I added, Or a different kind of noise. They can't help but yap and yelp, she said. I'll have to leave, I said. She found some old hangings in the family junk and hung them before our doors, hers and mine. I asked her if it would not be possible, now and then, to have a parsnip. A parsnip! she cried, as if I had asked for a dish of sucking Jew. I reminded her that the parsnip season was fast drawing to a close and that if, before it finally got there, she could feed me nothing but parsnips I'd be grateful. I like parsnips because they taste like violets and violets because they smell like parsnips. Were there no parsnips on earth violets would leave me cold and if violets did not exist I would care as little for parsnips as I do for turnips, or radishes. And even in the present state of their flora, I mean on this planet where parsnips and violets contrive to coexist, I could do without both with the utmost ease, the uttermost ease. One day she had the impudence to announce she was with child, and four or five months gone into the bargain, by me of all people! She offered me a side view of her belly. She even undressed, no doubt to prove she wasn't hiding a cushion under her skirt, and then of course for the pure pleasure of undressing. Perhaps it's just wind, I said, by way of consolation. She gazed at me with her big eyes whose colour I forget, with one big eye rather, for the other seemed riveted on the remains of the hyacinth. The more naked she was the more cross-eyed. Look, she said, stooping over her breasts, the haloes are darkening already. I summoned up my remaining strength and said, Abort, abort, and they'll blush like new. She had drawn back the curtain for a clear view of all her rotundities. I saw the mountain, impassible, cavernous, secret, where from morning to night I'd hear nothing but the wind, the curlews, the clink like distant silver of the stone-cutters' hammers. I'd come out in the day-time to the heather and gorse, all warmth and scent, and watch at night the distant city lights, if I chose, and the other lights, the lighthouses and lightships my father had named for me, when I was small, and whose names I could find again, in my memory, if I chose, that I knew. From that day forth things went from bad to worse, to worse and worse. Not that she neglected me, she could never have neglected me enough, but the way she kept plaguing me with *our* child, exhibiting her belly and breasts and saying it was due any moment, she could feel it lepping already. If it's lepping, I said, it's not mine. I might have been worse off than I was, in that house, that was certain, it fell short of my ideal naturally, but I wasn't blind to its advantages. I hesitated to leave, the leaves were falling already, I dreaded the winter. One should not dread the winter, it too has its bounties, the snow gives warmth and deadens the tumult and its pale days are soon over. But I did not yet know, at that time, how tender the earth can be for those who have only her and how many graves in her giving, for the living. What finished me was the birth. It woke me up. What that infant must have been going through! I fancy she had a woman with her, I seemed to hear steps in the kitchen, on and off. It went to my heart to leave a house without being put out. I crawled out over the back of the sofa, put on my coat, greatcoat and hat, I can think of nothing else, laced up my boots and opened the door to the corridor. A mass of junk barred my way, but I scrabbled and barged my way through it in the end, regardless of the clatter. I used the word marriage, it was a kind of union in spite of all. Precautions would have been superfluous, there was no competing with those cries. It must have been her first. They pursued me down the stairs and out into the street. I stopped before the house door and listened. I could still hear them. If I had not known there was crying in the house I might not have heard them. But knowing it I did. I was not sure where I was. I looked among the stars and constellations for the Wains, but could not find them. And yet they must have been there. My father was the first to show them to me. He had shown me others, but alone, without him beside me, I could never find any but the Wains. I began playing with the cries, a little in the same way as I had played with the song, on, back, on, back, if that may be called playing. As long as I kept walking I didn't hear them, because of the footsteps. But as soon as I halted I heard them again, a little fainter each time, admittedly, but what does it matter, faint or loud, cry is cry, all that matters is that it should cease. For years I thought they would cease. Now I don't think so any more. I could have done with other loves perhaps. But there it is, either you love or you don't.

M. R. JAMES *Canon Alberic's Scrap-Book*

JAMES JOYCE *Two Gallants*

FRANZ KAFKA *In the Penal Colony*

RUDYARD KIPLING *'They'*

D. H. LAWRENCE *Odour of Chrysanthemums*

PRIMO LEVI *The Magic Paint*

H. P. LOVECRAFT *The Colour Out Of Space*

MALCOLM LOWRY *Lunar Caustic*

CARSON MCCULLERS *Wunderkind*

KATHERINE MANSFIELD *Bliss*

ROBERT MUSIL *Flypaper*

VLADIMIR NABOKOV *Terra Incognita*

R. K. NARAYAN *A Breath of Lucifer*

FRANK O'CONNOR *The Cornet-Player Who Betrayed Ireland*

DOROTHY PARKER *The Sexes*

LUDMILLA PETRUSHEVSKAYA *Through the Wall*

JEAN RHYS *La Grosse Fifi*

SAKI *Filboid Studge, the Story of a Mouse That Helped*

ISAAC BASHEVIS SINGER *The Last Demon*

WILLIAM TREVOR *The Mark-2 Wife*

JOHN UPDIKE *Rich in Russia*

H. G. WELLS *The Door in the Wall*

EUDORA WELTY *Moon Lake*

P. G. WODEHOUSE *The Crime Wave at Blandings*

VIRGINIA WOOLF *The Lady in the Looking-Glass*

STEFAN ZWEIG *Chess*

a little history

Penguin Modern Classics were launched in 1961, and have been shaping the reading habits of generations ever since.

The list began with distinctive grey spines and evocative pictorial covers – a look that, after various incarnations, continues to influence their current design – and with books that are still considered landmark classics today.

Penguin Modern Classics have caused scandal and political change, inspired great films and broken down barriers, whether social, sexual or the boundaries of language itself. They remain the most provocative, groundbreaking, exciting and revolutionary works of the last 100 years (or so).

In 2011, on the fiftieth anniversary of the Modern Classics, we're publishing fifty Mini Modern Classics: the very best short fiction by writers ranging from Beckett to Conrad, Nabokov to Saki, Updike to Wodehouse. Though they don't take long to read, they'll stay with you long after you turn the final page.

MODERN CLASSICS
www.penguinclassics.com